BLUE ROSE

PETER STRAUB

BLUE ROSE

penguin books

PENGUIN BOOKS

Published by the Penguin Group

Penguin Books USA Inc., 375 Hudson Street,
New York, New York 10014, U.S.A.
Penguin Books Ltd, 27 Wrights Lane,
London W8 5TZ, England
Penguin Books Australia Ltd, Ringwood,
Victoria, Australia
Penguin Books Canada Ltd, 10 Alcorn Avenue,
Toronto, Ontario, Canada M4V 3B2
Penguin Books (N.Z.) Ltd, 182–190 Wairau Road,
Auckland 10, New Zealand

Penguin Books Ltd, Registered Offices:
Harmondsworth, Middlesex, England

Published in Penguin Books 1995

"Blue Rose" appears in Mr. Straub's *Houses Without Doors*,
published by Dutton Signet.

PUBLISHER'S NOTE

This is a work of fiction. Names, characters, places, and incidents are either the product of the author's imagination or are used fictitiously, and any resemblance to actual persons, living or dead, events, or locales is entirely coincidental.

ISBN 0 14 60.0107 9

Printed in the United States of America

for Rosemary Clooney

On a stifling summer day the two youngest of the five
Beevers children, Harry and Little Eddie, were sitting on
cane-backed chairs in the attic of their house on South
Sixth Street in Palmyra, New York. Their father called it
"the upstairs junk room," as this large irregular space was
reserved for the boxes of tablecloths, stacks of diminish-
ingly sized girls' winter coats, and musty old dresses
Maryrose Beevers had mummified as testimony to the su-
periority of her past to her present.

A tall mirror that could be tilted in its frame, an arti-
fact of their mother's onetime glory, now revealed to
Harry the rear of Little Eddie's head. This object, looking
more malleable than a head should be, was just peeking
above the back of the chair. Even the back of Little Eddie's head looked tense to Harry.

"Listen to me," Harry said. Little Eddie squirmed in
his chair, and the wobbly chair squirmed with him. "You
think I'm kidding you? I had her last year."

"Well, she didn't kill *you*," Little Eddie said.

" 'Course not, she liked me, you little dummy. She only 1

hit me a couple of times. She hit some of those kids every single day."

"But teachers can't *kill* people," Little Eddie said.

At nine, Little Eddie was only a year younger than he, but Harry knew that his undersized fretful brother saw him as much a part of the world of big people as their older brothers.

"Most teachers can't," Harry said. "But what if they live right in the same building as the principal? What if they won *teaching awards*, hey, and what if every other teacher in the place is scared stiff of them? Don't you think they can get away with murder? Do you think anybody really misses a snot-faced little brat—a little brat like you? Mrs. Franken took this kid, this runty little Tommy Golz, into the cloakroom, and she killed him right there. I heard him scream. At the end, it sounded just like bubbles. He was trying to yell, but there was too much blood in his throat. He never came back, and nobody ever said boo about it. She killed him, and next year she's going to be your teacher. I hope you're afraid, Little Eddie, because you ought to be." Harry leaned forward. "Tommy Golz even looked sort of like you, Little Eddie."

Little Eddie's entire face twitched as if a lightning bolt had crossed it.

In fact, the young Golz boy had suffered an epileptic fit and been removed from school, as Harry knew.

"Mrs. Franken especially hates selfish little brats that don't share their toys."

"I do share my toys," Little Eddie wailed, tears beginning to run down through the delicate smears of dust on his cheeks. "Everybody *takes* my toys, that's why."

"So give me your Ultraglide Roadster," Harry said. This had been Little Eddie's birthday present, given three days previous by a beaming father and a scowling mother. "Or I'll tell Mrs. Franken as soon as I get inside that school, this fall."

Under its layer of grime, Little Eddie's face went nearly the same white-gray shade as his hair.

An ominous slamming sound came up the stairs.

"Children? Are you messing around up there in the attic? Get down here!"

"We're just sitting in the chairs, Mom," Harry called out.

"Don't you bust those chairs! Get down here this minute!"

Little Eddie slid out of his chair and prepared to bolt.

"I want that car," Harry whispered. "And if you don't give it to me, I'll tell Mom you were foolin' around with her old clothes."

"I didn't do nothin'!" Little Eddie wailed, and broke for the stairs.

"Hey, Mom, we didn't break any stuff, honest!" Harry yelled. He bought a few minutes more by adding, "I'm coming right now," and stood up and went toward a cardboard box filled with interesting books he had noticed the day before his brother's birthday, and which had been his goal before he had remembered the Roadster and coaxed Little Eddie upstairs.

When, a short time later, Harry came through the door to the attic steps, he was carrying a tattered paperback book. Little Eddie stood quivering with misery and rage just outside the bedroom the two boys shared with their older brother Albert. He held out a small blue metal car, which Harry instantly took and eased into a front pocket of his jeans.

"When do I get it back?" Little Eddie asked.

"Never," Harry said. "Only selfish people want to get presents back. Don't you know anything at all?"

When Eddie pursed his face up to wail, Harry tapped the book in his hands and said, "I got something here that's going to help you with Mrs. Franken, so don't complain."

His mother intercepted him as he came down the stairs to the main floor of the little house—here were the kitchen and living room, both floored with faded linoleum, the actual "junk room" separated by a stiff brown woolen curtain from the little makeshift room where Edgar Beevers slept, and the larger bedroom reserved for Maryrose. Children were never permitted more than a few steps within this awful chamber, for they might disarrange Maryrose's mysterious "papers" or interfere with the rows of antique dolls on the window seat which was the sole, much-revered architectural distinction of the Beevers house.

Maryrose Beevers stood at the bottom of the stairs, glaring suspiciously up at her fourth son. She did not ever look like a woman who played with dolls, and she did not look that way now. Her hair was twisted into a knot at the back of her head. Smoke from her cigarette curled up past the big glasses like bird's wings, which magnified her eyes.

Harry thrust his hand into his pocket and curled his fingers protectively around the Ultraglide Roadster.

"Those things up there are the possessions of my family," she said. "Show me what you took."

Harry shrugged and held out the paperback as he came down within striking range.

His mother snatched it from him, and tilted her head to see its cover through the cigarette smoke. "Oh. This is from that little box of books up there? Your father used to pretend to read books." She squinted at the print on the cover. *"Hypnosis Made Easy.* Some drugstore trash. You want to read this?"

Harry nodded.

"I don't suppose it can hurt you much." She negligently passed the book back to him. "People in society read books, you know—I used to read a lot, back before I got stuck here with a bunch of dummies. *My* father had a lot of books."

Maryrose nearly touched the top of Harry's head, then snatched back her hand. "You're my scholar, Harry. You're the one who's going places."

"I'm gonna do good in school next year," he said.

"*Well*. You're going to do well. As long as you don't ruin every chance you have by speaking like your father."

Harry felt that particular pain composed of scorn, shame, and terror that filled him when Maryrose spoke of his father in this way. He mumbled something that sounded like acquiescence, and moved a few steps sideways and around her.

2

The porch of the Beevers house extended six feet on either side of the front door, and was the repository for furniture either too large to be crammed into the junk room or too humble to be enshrined in the attic. A sagging porch swing sat beneath the living room window, to the left of an ancient couch whose imitation green leather had been repaired with black duct tape; on the other side of the front door through which Harry Beevers now emerged stood a useless icebox dating from the earliest days of the Beeverses' marriage and two unsteady camp chairs Edgar Beevers had won in a card game. These had never been allowed into the house. Unofficially, this side of the porch was Harry's father's, and thereby had an entirely different atmosphere—defeated, lawless, and shameful—from the side with the swing and couch.

Harry knelt down in neutral territory directly before the front door and fished the Ultraglide Roadster from his pocket. He placed the hypnotism book on the porch and rolled the little metal car across its top. Then he gave the car a hard shove and watched it clunk nosedown onto the wood. He repeated this several times before moving the book aside, flattening himself out on his stomach, and giving the little car a decisive push toward the swing and the couch.

The Roadster rolled a few feet before an irregular board tilted it over on its side and stopped it.

"You dumb car," Harry said, and retrieved it. He gave it another push deeper into his mother's realm. A stiff, brittle section of paint which had separated from its board cracked in half and rested atop the stalled Roadster like a miniature mattress.

Harry knocked off the chip of paint and sent the car backward down the porch, where it flipped over again and skidded into the side of the icebox. The boy ran down the porch and this time simply hurled the little car back in the direction of the swing. It bounced off the swing's padding and fell heavily to the wood. Harry knelt before the icebox, panting.

His whole head felt funny, as if wet hot towels had been stuffed inside it. Harry picked himself up and walked across to where the car lay before the swing. He hated the way it looked, small and helpless. He experimentally stepped on the car and felt it pressing into the undersole of his moccasin. Harry raised his other foot and stood on the car, but nothing happened. He jumped on the car, but the moccasin was no better than his bare foot. Harry bent down to pick up the Roadster.

"You dumb little car," he said. "You're no good anyhow, you low-class little jerky thing." He turned it over in his hands. Then he inserted his thumbs between the frame and one of the little tires. When he pushed, the tire moved. His face heated. He mashed his thumbs against the tire, and the little black doughnut popped into the tall thick weeds in front of the porch. Breathing hard more from emotion than exertion, Harry popped the other front tire into the weeds. Harry whirled around, and ground the car into the wall beside his father's bedroom window. Long deep scratches appeared in the paint. When Harry peered at the top of the car, it too was scratched. He found a nail head which protruded a quarter of an inch out from the front of the house, and scraped a long paring of blue paint off the driver's side of the Roadster. Gray metal shone through. Harry slammed the car several times against the edge of the nail head, chipping off small quantities of paint. Panting, he popped off the two small rear tires and put them in his pocket because he liked the way they looked.

Without tires, well-scratched and dented, the Ultra-glide Roadster had lost most of its power. Harry looked it over with a bitter, deep satisfaction and walked across the porch and shoved it far into the nest of weeds. Gray metal and blue paint shone at him from within the stalks and leaves. Harry thrust his hands into their midst and swept his arms back and forth. The car tumbled away and fell into invisibility.

When Maryrose appeared scowling on the porch, Harry was seated serenely on the squeaking swing, looking at the first few pages of the paperback book.

"What are you doing? What was all that banging?"

"I'm just reading, I didn't hear anything," Harry said.

3

"Well, if it isn't the shitbird," Albert said, jumping up the porch steps thirty minutes later. His face and T-shirt bore broad black stripes of grease. A short, muscular thirteen-year-old, Albert spent every possible minute hanging around the gas station two blocks from their house. Harry knew that Albert despised him. Albert raised a fist and made a jerky, threatening motion toward Harry, who flinched. Albert had often beaten him bloody, as had their two older brothers, Sonny and George, now at Army bases in Oklahoma and Germany. Like Albert, his two oldest brothers had seriously disappointed their mother.

Albert laughed, and this time swung his fist within a couple of inches of Harry's face. On the backswing he knocked the book from Harry's hands.

"Thanks," Harry said.

Albert smirked and disappeared around the front door. Almost immediately Harry could hear his mother beginning to shout about the grease on Albert's face and clothes. Albert thumped up the stairs.

Harry opened his clenched fingers and spread them wide, closed his hands into fists, then spread them wide again. When he heard the bedroom door slam shut upstairs, he was able to get off the swing and pick up the book. Being around Albert made him feel like a spring coiled up in a box. From the upper rear of the house, Little Eddie emitted a ghostly wail. Maryrose screamed that she was going to start smacking him if he didn't shut up, and that was that. The three unhappy lives within the house fell back into silence. Harry sat down, found his page, and began reading again.

A man named Dr. Roland Mentaine had written *Hypnosis Made Easy*, and his vocabulary was much larger than Harry's. Dr. Mentaine used words like "orchestrate" and "ineffable" and "enhance," and some of his sentences wound their way through so many subordinate clauses that Harry lost his way. Yet Harry, who had begun the book only half-expecting that he would comprehend anything in it at all, found it a wonderful book. He had made it most of the way through the chapter call "Mind Power."

Harry thought it was neat that hypnosis could cure smoking, stuttering, and bed-wetting. (He himself had wet the bed almost nightly until months after his ninth birthday. The bed-wetting stopped the night a certain lovely dream came to Harry. In the dream he had to urinate terribly, and was hurrying down a stony castle corridor past suits of armor and torches guttering on the walls. At last Harry reached an open door, through which he saw the most splendid bathroom of his life. The floors were of polished marble, the walls white-tiled. As soon as he entered the gleaming bathroom, a uniformed butler waved him toward the rank of urinals. Harry began pulling down his zipper, fumbled with himself, and got his penis out of his underpants just in time. As the dream-urine gushed out of him, Harry had blessedly awakened.) Hypnotism 11 could get you right inside someone's mind and let you do things there. You could make a person speak in any foreign language they'd ever heard, even if they'd only heard it once, and you could make them act like a baby. Harry considered how pleasurable it would be to make his brother Albert lie squalling and red-faced on the floor, unable to walk or speak as he pissed all over himself.

Also, and this was a new thought to Harry, you could take a person back to a whole row of lives they had led before they were born as the person they were now. This process of rebirth was called reincarnation. Some of Dr. Mentaine's patients had been kings in Egypt and pirates in the Caribbean, some had been murderers, novelists, and artists. They remembered the houses they'd lived in, the names of their mothers and servants and children, the locations of shops where they'd bought cake and wine. Neat stuff, Harry thought. He wondered if someone who had been a famous murderer a long time ago could remember pushing in the knife or bringing down the hammer. A lot of the books remaining in the little cardboard box upstairs, Harry had noticed, seemed to be about murderers. It would not be any use to take Albert back to a previous life, however. If Albert had any previous lives, he had spent them as inanimate objects on the order of boulders and anvils.

Maybe in another life Albert was a murder weapon,
Harry thought.

"Hey, college boy! Joe College!"

Harry looked toward the sidewalk and saw the baseball cap and T-shirted gut of Mr. Petrosian, who lived in a tiny house next to the tavern on the corner of South Sixth and Livermore Street. Mr. Petrosian was always shouting genial things at kids, but Maryrose wouldn't let Harry or Little Eddie talk to him. She said Mr. Petrosian was common as dirt. He worked as a janitor in the telephone building and drank a case of beer every night while he sat on his porch.

"Me?" Harry said.

"Yeah! Keep reading books, and you could go to college, right?"

Harry smiled noncommittally. Mr. Petrosian lifted a wide arm and continued to toil down the street toward his house next to the Idle Hour.

In seconds Maryrose burst through the door, folding an old white dish towel in her hands. "Who was that? I heard a man's voice."

"Him," Harry said, pointing at the substantial back of Mr. Petrosian, now half of the way home.

"What did he say? As if it could possibly be interesting, coming from an Armenian janitor."

"He called me Joe College."

Maryrose startled him by smiling.

"Albert says he wants to go back to the station tonight, and I have to go to work soon." Maryrose worked the night shift as a secretary at St. Joseph's Hospital. "God knows when your father'll show up. Get something to eat for Little Eddie and yourself, will you, Harry? I've just got too many things to take care of, as usual."

"I'll get something at Big John's." This was a hamburger stand, a magical place to Harry, erected the summer before in a vacant lot on Livermore Street two blocks down from the Idle Hour.

His mother handed him two carefully folded dollar bills, and he pushed them into his pocket. "Don't let Little Eddie stay in the house alone," his mother said before going back inside. "Take him with you. You know how scared he gets."

"Sure," Harry said, and went back to his book. He finished the chapter on "Mind Power" while first Maryrose left to stand up at the bus stop on the corner, and then while Albert noisily departed. Little Eddie sat frozen before his soap operas in the living room. Harry turned a page and started reading "Techniques of Hypnosis."

4

At eight-thirty that night the two boys sat alone in the

kitchen, on opposite sides of the table covered in yellow

bamboo Formica. From the living room came the sound of Sid Caesar babbling in fake German to Imogene Coca on "Your Show of Shows." Little Eddie claimed to be scared of Sid Caesar, but when Harry had returned from the hamburger stand with a Big Johnburger (with "the works") for himself and a Mama Marydog for Eddie, double fries, and two chocolate shakes, he had been sitting in front of the television, his face moist with tears of mortal outrage. Eddie usually liked Mama Marydogs, but he had taken only a couple of meager bites from the one before him now, and was disconsolately pushing a french fry through a blob of ketchup. Every now and then he wiped at his eyes, leaving nearly symmetrical smears of ketchup to dry on his cheeks.

"Mom *said* not to leave me alone in the house," said Little Eddie. "I heard. It was during 'The Edge of Night' and you were on the porch. I think I'm gonna tell on you." He peeped across at Harry, then quickly looked back at the french fry and drew it out of the puddle of ketchup. "I'm ascared to be alone in the house." Sometimes Eddie's voice was like a queer speeded-up mechanical version of Maryrose's.

"Don't be so dumb," Harry said, almost kindly. "How can you be scared in your own house? You live here, don't you?"

"I'm ascared of the attic," Eddie said. He held the dripping french fry before his mouth and pushed it in. 15

"The attic makes noise." A little squirm of red appeared at the corner of his mouth. "You were supposed to take me with you."

"Oh, jeez, Eddie, you slow everything down. I wanted to just get the food and come back. I got you your dinner, didn't I? Didn't I get you what you like?"

In truth, Harry liked hanging around Big John's by himself because then he could talk to Big John and listen to his theories. Big John called himself a "renegade Papist" and considered Hitler the greatest man of the twentieth century, followed closely by Paul XI, Padre Pio who bled from the palms of his hands, and Elvis Presley.

All these events occurred in what is usually but wrongly called a simpler time, before Kennedy and feminism and ecology, before the Nixon presidency and Watergate, and before American soldiers, among them a twenty-one-year-old Harry Beevers, journeyed to Vietnam.

"I'm still going to tell," said Little Eddie. He pushed another french fry into the puddle of ketchup. "And that car was my birthday present." He began to snuffle. "Albert hit me, and you stole my car, and you left me alone, and I was scared. And I don't wanna have Mrs. Franken next year, cuz I think she's gonna hurt me."

Harry had nearly forgotten telling his brother about Mrs. Franken and Tommy Golz, and this reminder brought back very sharply the memory of destroying Eddie's birthday present.

Eddie twisted his head sideways and dared another quick look at his brother. "Can I have my Ultraglide Roadster back, Harry? You're going to give it back to me aren'cha? I won't tell Mom you left me alone if you give it back."

"Your car is okay," Harry said. "It's in a sort of a secret place I know."

"You hurt my car?" Eddie squalled. "You did!"

"Shut up!" Harry shouted, and Little Eddie flinched. "You're driving me crazy!" Harry yelled. He realized that he was leaning over the table, and that Little Eddie was getting ready to cry again. He sat down. "Just don't scream at me like that, Eddie."

"You did something to my car," Eddie said with a stunned certainty. "I knew it."

"Look, I'll prove your car is okay," Harry said, and took the two rear tires from his pocket and displayed them on his palm.

Little Eddie stared. He blinked, then reached out tentatively for the tires.

Harry closed his fist around them. "Do they look like I did anything to them?"

"You took them *off!*"

"But don't they look okay, don't they look fine?" Harry opened his fist, closed it again, and returned the tires to his pocket. "I didn't want to show you the whole car, Eddie, because you'd get all worked up, and you gave it to 17 me. Remember? I wanted to show you the tires so you'd see everything was all right. Okay? Got it?"

Eddie miserably shook his head.

"Anyway, I'm going to help you, just like I said."

"With Mrs. Franken?" A fraction of his misery left Little Eddie's smeary face.

"Sure. You ever hear of something called hypnotism?"

"I heard a hypmotism." Little Eddie was sulking. "Everybody in the whole world heard a that."

"Hypnotism, stupid, not hypmotism."

"Sure, hypmotism. I saw it on the TV. They did it on 'As the World Turns.' A man made a lady go to sleep and think she was going to have a baby."

Harry smiled. "That's just TV, Little Eddie. Real hypnotism is a lot better than that. I read all about it in one of the books from the attic."

Little Eddie was sulky because of the car. "So what makes it better?"

"Because it lets you do amazing things," Harry said. He called on Dr. Mentaine. "Hypnosis unlocks your mind and lets you use all the power you really have. If you start now, you'll really knock those books when school starts up again. You'll pass every test Mrs. Franken gives you, just like the way I did." He reached across the table and grasped Little Eddie's wrist, stalling a fat brown french fry on its way to the puddle. "But it won't just make you good in school. If you let me try it on you, I'm pretty sure I can show you that you're a lot stronger than you think you are."

Eddie blinked.

"And I bet I can make you so you're not scared of anything anymore. Hypnotism is real good for that. I read in this book, there was this guy who was afraid of bridges. Whenever he even *thought* about crossing a bridge he got all dizzy and sweaty. Terrible stuff happened to him, like he lost his job and once he just had to ride in a car across a bridge and he dumped a load in his pants. He went to see Dr. Mentaine, and Dr. Mentaine hypnotized him and said he would never be afraid of bridges again, and he wasn't."

Harry pulled the paperback from his hip pocket. He opened it flat on the table and bent over the pages. "Here. Listen to this. 'Benefits of the course of treatment were found in all areas of the patient's life, and results were obtained for which he would have paid any price." Harry read these words haltingly, but with complete understanding.

"Hypmotism can make me strong?" Little Eddie asked, evidently having saved this point in his head.

"Strong as a bull."

"Strong as Albert?"

"A lot stronger than Albert. A lot stronger than me, too."

"And I can beat up on big guys that hurt me?"

"You just have to learn how."

Eddie sprang up from the chair, yelling nonsense. He flexed his stringlike biceps and for some time twisted his body into a series of muscleman poses.

"You want to do it?" Harry finally asked.

Little Eddie popped into his chair and stared at Harry. His T-shirt's neck band sagged all the way to his breastbone without ever actually touching his chest. "I wanna start."

"Okay, Eddie, good man." Harry stood up and put his hand on the book. "Up to the attic."

"Only, I don't wanna go in the attic," Eddie said. He was still staring at Harry, but his head was tilted over like a weird little echo of Maryrose, and his eyes had filled with suspicion.

"I'm not gonna *take* anything from you, Little Eddie," Harry said. "It's just, we should be out of everybody's way. The attic's real quiet."

Little Eddie stuck his hand inside his T-shirt and let his arm dangle from the wrist.

"You turned your shirt into an armrest," Harry said.

Eddie jerked his hand out of its sling.

"Albert might come waltzing in and wreck everything if we do it in the bedroom."

"If you go up first and turn on the lights," Eddie said.

5

Harry held the book open on his lap, and glanced from it to Little Eddie's tense smeary face. He had read these pages over many times while he sat on the porch. Hypnotism boiled down to a few simple steps, each of which led to the next. The first thing he had to do was to get his brother started right, "relaxed and receptive," according to Dr. Mentaine.

Little Eddie stirred in his cane-backed chair and kneaded his hands together. His shadow, cast by the bulb dangling overhead, imitated him like a black little chair-bound monkey. "I wanna get started, I wanna get to be strong," he said.

"Right here in this book it says you have to be relaxed," Harry said. "Just put your hands on top of your legs, nice and easy, with your fingers pointing forward. Then close your eyes and breathe in and out a couple of times. Think about being nice and tired and ready to go to sleep."

"I don't wanna go to sleep!"

"It's not really sleep, Little Eddie, it's just sort of like it. You'll still really be awake, but nice and relaxed. Or else it won't work. You have to do everything I tell you. Otherwise everybody'll still be able to beat up on you, like they do now. I want you to pay attention to everything I say."

"Okay." Little Eddie made a visible effort to relax. He placed his hands on his thighs and twice inhaled and exhaled.

"Now close your eyes."

Eddie closed his eyes.

Harry suddenly knew that it was going to work—if he did everything the book said, he would really be able to hypnotize his brother.

"Little Eddie, I want you just to listen to the sound of my voice," he said, forcing himself to be calm. "You are already getting nice and relaxed, as easy and peaceful as if you were lying in bed, and the more you listen to my voice the more relaxed and tired you are going to get. Nothing can bother you. Everything bad is far away, and you're just sitting here, breathing in and out, getting nice and sleepy."

He checked his page to make sure he was doing it right, and then went on.

"It's like lying in bed, Eddie, and the more you hear my voice the more tired and sleepy you're getting, a little more sleepy the more you hear me. Everything else is sort of fading away, and all you can hear is my voice. You feel

tired but good, just like the way you do right before you

fall asleep. Everything is fine, and you're drifting a little bit, drifting and drifting, and you're getting ready to raise your right hand."

He leaned over and very lightly stroked the back of Little Eddie's grimy right hand. Eddie sat slumped in the chair with his eyes closed, breathing shallowly. Harry spoke very slowly.

"I'm going to count backward from ten, and every time I get to another number, your hand is going to get lighter and lighter. When I count, your right hand is going to get so light it floats up and finally touches your nose when you hear me say 'One.' And then you'll be in a deep sleep. Now I'm starting. Ten. Your hand is already feeling light. Nine. It wants to float up. Eight. Your hand really feels light now. It's going to start to go up now. Seven."

Little Eddie's hand obediently floated an inch up from his thigh.

"Six." The grimy little hand rose another few inches. "It's getting lighter and lighter now, and every time I say another number it gets closer and closer to your nose, and you get sleepier and sleepier. Five."

The hand ascended several inches nearer Eddie's face.

"Four."

The hand now dangled like a sleeping bird half of the way between Eddie's knee and his nose.

"Three."

It rose nearly to Eddie's chin.

"Two."

Eddie's hand hung a few inches from his mouth.

"One. You are going to fall asleep now."

The gently curved, ketchup-streaked forefinger delicately brushed the tip of Little Eddie's nose, and stayed there while Eddie sagged against the back of the chair.

Harry's heart beat so loudly that he feared the sound would bring Eddie out of his trance. Eddie remained motionless. Harry breathed quietly by himself for a moment. "Now you can lower your hand to your lap, Eddie. You are going deeper and deeper into sleep. Deeper and deeper and deeper."

Eddie's hand sank gracefully downward.

The attic seemed hot as the inside of a furnace to Harry. His fingers left blotches on the open pages of the book. He wiped his face on his sleeve and looked at his little brother. Little Eddie had slumped so far down in the chair that his head was no longer visible in the tilting mirror. Perfectly still and quiet, the attic stretched out on all sides of them, waiting (or so it seemed to Harry) for what would happen next. Maryrose's trunks sat in rows under the eaves far behind the mirror, her old dresses hung silently within the dusty wardrobe. Harry rubbed his hands on his jeans to dry them, and flicked a page over with the neatness of an old scholar who had spent half his life in libraries.

24   "You're going to sit up straight in your chair," he said.

Eddie pulled himself upright.

"Now I want to show you that you're really hypnotized, Little Eddie. It's like a test. I want you to hold your right arm straight out before you. Make it as rigid a you can. This is going to show you how strong you can be."

Eddie's pale arm rose and straightened to the wrist, leaving his fingers dangling. '

Harry stood up and said, "That's pretty good." He walked the two steps to Eddie's side and grasped his brother's arm and ran his fingers down the length of it, gently straightening Eddie's hand. "Now I want you to imagine that your arm is getting harder and harder. It's getting as hard and rigid as an iron bar. Your whole arm is an iron bar, and nobody on earth could bend it. Eddie, it's stronger than Superman's arm." He removed his hands and stepped back.

"Now. This arm is so strong and rigid that you can't bend it no matter how hard you try. It's an iron bar, and nobody on earth could bend it. Try. Try to bend it."

Eddie's face tightened up, and his arm rose perhaps two degrees. Eddie grunted with invisible effort, unable to bend his arm.

"Okay, Eddie, you did real good. Now your arm is loosening up, and when I count backward from ten, it's going to get looser and looser. When I get to *one*, your arm'll be normal again." He began counting, and Eddie's fingers 25 loosened and dropped, and finally the arm came to rest again on his leg.

Harry went back to his chair, sat down, and looked at Eddie with great satisfaction. Now he was certain that he would be able to do the next demonstration, which Dr. Mentaine called "The Chair Exercise."

"Now you know that this stuff really works, Eddie, so we're going to do something a little harder. I want you to stand up in front of your chair."

Eddie obeyed. Harry stood up too, and moved his chair forward and to the side so that its cane seat faced Eddie, about four feet away.

"I want you to stretch out between these chairs, with your head on your chair and your feet on mine. And I want you to keep your hands at your sides."

Eddie hunkered down uncomplainingly and settled his head back on the seat of his chair. Supporting himself with his arms, he raised one leg and placed his foot on Harry's chair. Then he lifted the other foot. Difficulty immediately appeared in his face. He raised his arms and clamped them in so that he looked trussed.

"Now your whole body is slowly becoming as hard as iron, Eddie. Your entire body is one of the strongest things on earth. Nothing can make it bend. You could hold yourself there forever and never feel the slightest pain or discomfort. It's like you're lying on a mattress, 26 you're so strong."

The expression of strain left Eddie's face. Slowly his arms extended and relaxed. He lay propped string-straight between the two chairs, so at ease that he did not even appear to be breathing.

"While I talk to you, you're getting stronger and stronger. You could hold up anything. You could hold up an elephant. I'm going to sit down on your stomach to prove it."

Cautiously, Harry seated himself down on his brother's midriff. He raised his legs. Nothing happened. After he had counted slowly to fifteen, Harry lowered his legs and stood. "I'm going to take my shoes off now, Eddie, and stand on you."

He hurried over to a piano stool embroidered with fulsome roses and carried it back; then he slipped off his moccasins and stepped on top of the stool. As Harry stepped on top of Eddie's exposed thin belly, the chair supporting his brother's head wobbled. Harry stood stock-still for a moment, but the chair held. He lifted the other foot from the stool. No movement from the chair. He set the other foot on his brother. Little Eddie effortlessly held him up.

Harry lifted himself experimentally up on his toes and came back down on his heels. Eddie seemed entirely unaffected. Then Harry jumped perhaps half an inch into the air, and since Eddie did not even grunt when he landed, he kept jumping, five, six, seven, eight times, until he was breathing hard. "You're amazing Little Eddie," he said, and stepped off onto the stool. "Now you can begin to relax. You can put your feet on the floor. Then I want you to sit back up in your chair. Your body doesn't feel stiff anymore."

Little Eddie had been rather tentatively lowering one foot, but as soon as Harry finished speaking he buckled in the middle and thumped his bottom on the floor. Harry's chair (Maryrose's chair) sickeningly tipped over, but landed soundlessly on a neat woolen stack of layered winter coats.

Moving like a robot, Little Eddie slowly sat upright on the floor. His eyes were open but unfocused.

"You can stand up now and get back in your chair," Harry said. He did not remember leaving the stool, but he had left it. Sweat ran into his eyes. He pressed his face into his shirtsleeve. For a second, panic had brightly beckoned. Little Eddie was sleepwalking back to his chair. When he sat down, Harry said, "Close your eyes. You're going deeper and deeper into sleep. Deeper and deeper, Little Eddie."

Eddie settled into the chair as if nothing had happened, and Harry reverently set his own chair upright again. Then he picked up the book and opened it. The print swam before his eyes. Harry shook his head and looked 28 again, but still the lines of print snaked across the page.

He pressed the palms of his hands against his eyes, and red patterns exploded across his vision.

He removed his hands from his eyes, blinked, and found that although the lines of print were now behaving themselves, he no longer wanted to go on. The attic was too hot, he was too tired, and the toppling of the chair had been too close a brush with actual disaster. But for a time he leafed purposefully through the book while Eddie tranced on, and then found the subheading "Posthypnotic Suggestion."

"Little Eddie, we're just going to do one more thing. If we ever do this again, it'll help us go faster." Harry shut the book. He knew exactly how this went; he would even use the same phrase Dr. Mentaine used with his patients. *Blue rose*—Harry did not quite know why, but he liked the sound of that.

"I'm going to tell you a phrase, Eddie, and from now on whenever you hear me say this phrase, you will instantly go back to sleep and be hypnotized again. The phrase is 'Blue rose.' Blue rose. When you hear me say 'Blue rose,' you will go right to sleep, just the way you are now, and we can make you stronger again. 'Blue rose' is our secret, Eddie, because nobody else knows it. What is it?"

"Blue rose," Eddie said in a muffled voice.

"Okay. I'm going to count backward from ten, and when I get to 'one' you will be wide awake again. You will not remember anything we did, but you will feel happy and strong. Ten."

As Harry counted backward, Little Eddie twitched and stirred, let his arms fall to his sides, thumped one foot carelessly on the floor, and at "one" opened his eyes.

"Did it work? What'd I do? Am I strong?"

"You're a bull," Harry said. "It's getting late, Eddie— time to go downstairs."

Harry's timing was accurate enough to be uncomfortable. As soon as the two boys closed the attic door behind them they heard the front door slide open in a cacophony of harsh coughs and subdued mutterings followed by the sound of unsteady footsteps proceeding to the bathroom. Edgar Beevers was home.

6

Late that night the three homebound Beevers sons lay in their separate beds in the good-sized second-floor room next to the attic stairs. Directly above Maryrose's bedroom, its dimensions were nearly identical to it except that the boy's room, the "dorm," had no window seat and the attic stairs shaved a couple of feet from Harry's end. When the other two boys had lived at home, Harry and

Little Eddie had slept together, Albert had slept in a bed with Sonny, and only George, who at the time of his induction into the Army had been six feet tall and weighed two hundred and one pounds, had slept alone. In those days, Sonny had often managed to make Albert cry out in the middle of the night. The very idea of George could still make Harry's stomach freeze.

Though it was now very late, enough light from the street came in through the thin white net curtains to give complex shadows to the bunched muscles of Albert's upper arms as he lay stretched out atop his sheets. The voices of Maryrose and Edgar Beevers, one approximately sober and the other unmistakably drunk, came clearly up the stairs and through the open door.

"*Who* says I waste my time? I don't say that. I don't waste my time."

"I suppose you think you've done a good day's work when you spell a bartender for a couple of hours—and then drink up your wages! That's the story of your life, Edgar Beevers, and it's a sad sad story of W-A-S-T-E. If my father could have seen what would become of you . . ."

"I ain't so damn bad."

"You ain't so damn good, either."

"Albert," Eddie said softly from his bed between his two brothers.

As if galvanized by Little Eddie's voice, Albert suddenly sat up in bed, leaned forward, and reached out to try to smack Eddie with his fist.

"I didn't do nothin'!" Harry said, and moved to the edge of his mattress. The blow had been for him, he knew, not Eddie, except that Albert was too lazy to get up.

"I hate your lousy guts," Albert said. "If I wasn't too tired to get out of this here bed, I'd pound your face in."

"Harry stole my birthday car, Albert," Eddie said. "Makum gimme it back."

"One day," Maryrose said from downstairs, "at the end of the summer when I was seventeen, late in the afternoon, my father said to my mother, 'Honey, I believe I'm going to take out our pretty little Maryrose and get her something special,' and he called up to me from the drawing room to make myself pretty and get set to go, and because my father was a gentleman and a Man of His Word, I got ready in two shakes. My father was wearing a very handsome brown suit and a red bow tie and his boater. I remember just like I can see it now. He stood at the bottom of the staircase, waiting for me, and when I came down he took my arm and we just went out that front door like a courting couple. Down the stone walk, which my father put in all by himself even though he was a white-collar worker, down Majeski Street, arm in arm down to South Palmyra Avenue. In those days all the best people, all the people who counted, did their shopping on
32 South Palmyra Avenue."

"I'd like to knock your teeth down your throat," Albert said to Harry.

"Albert, he took my birthday car, he really did, and I want it back. I'm ascared he busted it. I want it back so much I'm gonna die."

Albert propped himself up on an elbow and for the first time really looked at Little Eddie. Eddie whimpered. "You're such a twerp," Albert said. "I wish you *would* die, Eddie, I wish you'd just drop dead so we could stick you in the ground and forget about you. I wouldn't even cry at your funeral. Prob'ly I wouldn't even be able to remember your name. I'd just say, 'Oh, yeah, he was that little creepy kid used to hang around cryin' all the time, glad he's dead, whatever his name was.' "

Eddie had turned his back on Albert and was weeping softly, his unwashed face distorted by the shadows into an uncanny image of the mask of tragedy.

"You know, I really wouldn't mind if you dropped dead," Albert mused. "You neither, shitbird."

". . . realized he was taking me to Allouette's. I'm sure you used to look in their windows when you were a little boy. You remember Allouette's, don't you? There's never been anything so beautiful as that store. When I was a little girl and lived in the big house, all the best people used to go there. My father marched me right inside, with his arm around me, and took me up in the elevator and we went straight to the lady who managed the dress depart- 33 ment. 'Give my little girl the best,' he said. Price was no object. Quality was all he cared about. 'Give my little girl the best.' *Are you listening to me, Edgar?*"

Albert snored face-down into his pillow; Little Eddie twitched and snuffled. Harry lay awake for so long he thought he would never get to sleep. Before him he kept seeing Little Eddie's face all slack and dopey under hypnosis—Little Eddie's face made him feel hot and uncomfortable. Now that Harry was lying down in bed, it seemed to him that everything he had done since returning from Big John's seemed really to have been done by someone else, or to have been done in a dream. Then he realized that he had to use the bathroom.

Harry slid out of bed, quietly crossed the room, went out onto the dark landing, and felt his way downstairs to the bathroom.

When he emerged, the bathroom light showed him the squat black shape of the telephone atop the Palmyra directory. Harry moved to the low telephone table beside the stairs. He lifted the phone from the directory and opened the book, the width of a Big 5 tablet, with his other hand. As he had done on many other nights when his bladder forced him downstairs, Harry leaned over the page and selected a number. He kept the number in his head as he closed the directory and replaced the telephone. He dialed. The number rang so often Harry lost count. At last a hoarse voice answered. Harry said, "I'm watching you, and you're a dead man." He softly replaced the receiver in the cradle.

7

Harry caught up with his father the next afternoon just as Edgar Beevers had begun to move up South Sixth Street toward the corner of Livermore. His father wore his usual costume of baggy gray trousers cinched far above his waist by a belt with a double buckle, a red-and-white plaid shirt, and a brown felt hat stationed low over his eyes. His long fleshy nose swam before him, cut in half by the shadow of the hat brim.

"Dad!"

His father glanced incuriously at him, then put his hands back in his pockets. He turned sideways and kept walking down the street, though perhaps a shade more slowly. "What's up kid? No school?"

"It's summer, there isn't any school. I just thought I'd come with you for a little."

"Well, I ain't doing much. Your ma asked me to pick up some hamburg on Livermore, and I thought I'd slip 35 into the Idle Hour for a quick belt. You won't turn me in, will you?"

"No."

"You ain't a bad kid, Harry. Your ma's just got a lot of worries. I worry about Little Eddie too, sometimes."

"Sure."

"What's with the books? You read when you walk?"

"I was just sort of looking at them," Harry said.

His father insinuated his hand beneath Harry's left elbow and extracted two luridly jacketed paperback books. They were titled *Murder, Incorporated* and *Hitler's Death Camps*. Harry already loved both of these books. His father grunted and handed *Murder, Incorporated* back to him. He raised the other book nearly to the top of his nose and peered at the cover, which depicted a naked woman pressing herself against a wall of barbed wire while a uniformed Nazi aimed a rifle at her back.

Looking up at his father, Harry saw that beneath the harsh line of shadow cast by the hat brim, his father's whiskers grew in different colors and patterns. Black and brown, red and orange, the glistening spikes swirled across his father's cheek.

"I bought this book, but it didn't look nothing like that," his father said, and returned the book.

"What didn't?"

"That place. Dachau. That death camp."

"How do you know?"

"I was there, wasn't I? You wasn't even born then. It didn't look anything like that picture on that book. It just looked like a piece a shit to me, like most of the places I saw when I was in the Army."

This was the first time Harry had heard that his father had been in the service.

"You mean, you were in World War II?"

"Yeah, I was in the Big One. They made me corporal over there. Had me a nickname, too. 'Beans.' 'Beans' Beevers. And I got a Purple Heart from the time I got a infection."

"You saw Dachau with your own eyes?"

"Damn straight I did." He bent down suddenly. "Hey—don't let your ma catch you readin' that book."

Secretly pleased, Harry shook his head. Now the book and the death camp were a bond between himself and his father.

"Did you ever kill anybody?"

His father wiped his mouth and both cheeks with one long hand. Harry saw a considering eye far back in the shadow of the brim.

"I killed a guy once."

A long pause.

"I shot him in the back."

His father wiped his mouth again, and then motioned forward with his head. He had to get to the bar, the butcher, and back again in a very carefully defined period of time. "You really want to hear this?"

Harry nodded. He swallowed.

"I guess you do, at that. Okay—we was sent into this camp, Dachau, at the end of the war to process the prisoners and arrest the guards and the commandant. Everything was all arranged. A bunch of brass hats from Division were going to come on an inspection, so we had to wait there a couple days. We had these guards lined up, see, and these skinny old wrecks would come up and give 'em hell. We wasn't supposed to let 'em get too near."

They were passing Mr. Petrosian's little tar-paper house, and Harry felt a spasm of relief that Mr. Petrosian was not out on his tiny porch, working on his case of beer. The Idle Hour was only a few paces ahead.

"Anyhow, one of these guards, one of the worst ones, suddenly decided he's going to run for it. He takes off, runnin' like crazy toward the woods. What do I do? I ask. Nobody knows what the hell to do. Shoot him, somebody says. So I shot him in the back. That was all she wrote."

Now they had reached the screen door that led into the Idle Hour, and the smells of malt and hops filled the air. "See you back at the house," his father said, and disappeared through the screen door like a magician.

After Harry had read a hundred pages of *Murder, Incorporated*, his favorite murderers were Louis "Lepke" Buchalter and Abe "Kid Twist" Reles. They were dependable professionals. A kind of black light surrounded them and made them glitter. Lepke Buchalter and Abe Reles looked out at the world from the shadows of their hat brims. They lived in shadowy rooms and peered out through the curtains. They appeared on a dark corner before their terrified victim, did their work, and walked away, turning up their coat collars.

Suppose you had some kind of job that took you around the country, like a salesman's job, Harry thought as he read away the afternoon in the porch swing; suppose you had a job that took you from one town to another. Suppose you killed someone in each one of those towns, carefully and quietly, and hid the bodies so it would take people a long time to find them. Your work would never be done.

"Blue rose," Harry said.

Little Eddie sagged openmouthed against the cane of his chair, his hands loose in his lap.

It had worked. Harry looked around as if he expected applause, and did feel that all the things in the attic looked back at him with warm approval. It was nine-thirty at night; he and Eddie, alone in the house, occupied the attic in perfect safety. Harry wanted to see if he could put other people under and make them do things, but for now, for tonight, he was content to experiment with Eddie.

"You're going deeper and deeper asleep, Eddie, deeper and deeper, and you're listening to every word I say. You're just sinking down and down, hearing my voice come to you, going deeper and deeper with every word, and now you are real deep asleep and ready to begin."

Little Eddie sat sprawled over Maryrose's canebacked chair, his chin touching his chest and his little pink mouth drooping open. He looked like a slightly under-sized seven-year-old, like a second-grader instead of the 40 fourth-grader he would be when he joined Mrs. Franken's class in the fall. Suddenly he reminded Harry of the Ultraglide Roadster, scratched and dented and stripped of its tires.

"Tonight you're going to see how strong you really are. Sit up, Eddie."

Eddie pulled himself upright and closed his mouth, almost comically obedient.

Harry thought it would be fun to make Little Eddie believe he was a dog and trot around the attic on all fours, barking and lifting his leg. Then he saw Little Eddie staggering across the attic, his tongue bulging out of his mouth, his own hands squeezing and squeezing his throat. Maybe he would try that too, after he had done several other exercises he had discovered in Dr. Mentaine's book. He checked the underside of his collar for maybe the fifth time that evening, and felt the long thin shaft of the pearl-headed hat pin he had stopped reading *Murder, Incorporated* long enough to smuggle out of Maryrose's bedroom after she had left for work.

"Eddie," he said,"now you are very deeply asleep, and you will be able to do everything I say. I want you to hold your right arm straight out in from of you."

Eddie stuck his arm out like a poker.

"That's good, Eddie. Now I want you to notice that all the feeling is leaving that arm. It's getting number and number. It doesn't even feel like flesh and blood anymore. It feels like it's made out of steel or something. It's so 41 numb that you can't feel anything there anymore. You can't even feel pain in it."

Harry stood up, went toward Eddie, and brushed his fingers along his arm. "You didn't feel anything, did you?"

"No," Eddie said in a slow gravel-filled voice.

"Do you feel anything now?" Harry pinched the underside of Eddie's forearm.

"No."

"Now?" Harry used his nails to pinch the side of Eddie's bicep, hard, and left purple dents in the skin.

"No," Eddie repeated.

"How about this?" He slapped his hand against Eddie's forearm as hard as he could. There was a sharp loud smacking sound, and his fingers tingled. If Little Eddie had not been hypnotized, he would have tried to screech down the walls.

"No," Eddie said.

Harry pulled the hat pin out of his collar and inspected his brother's arm. "You're doing great, Little Eddie. You're stronger than anybody in your whole class—you're probably stronger than the whole rest of the school." He turned Eddie's arm so that the palm was up and the white forearm, lightly traced by small blue veins, faced him.

Harry delicately ran the point of the hat pin down Eddie's pale, veined forearm. The pinpoint left a narrow
42 chalk-white scratch in its wake. For a moment Harry felt

the floor of the attic sway beneath his feet; then he closed his eyes and jabbed the hat pin into Little Eddie's skin as hard as he could.

He opened his eyes. The floor was still swaying beneath him. From Little Eddie's lower arm protruded six inches of the eight-inch hat pin, the mother-of-pearl head glistening softly in the light from the overhead bulb. A drop of blood the size of a watermelon seed stood on Eddie's skin. Harry moved back to his chair and sat down heavily. "Do you feel anything?"

"No," Eddie said again in that surprisingly deep voice.

Harry stared at the hat pin embedded in Eddie's arm. The oval drop of blood lengthened itself out against the white skin and began slowly to ooze toward Eddie's wrist. Harry watched it advance across the pale underside of Eddie's forearm. Finally he stood up and returned to Eddie's side. The elongated drop of blood had ceased moving. Harry bent over and twanged the hat pin. Eddie could feel nothing. Harry put his thumb and forefinger on the glistening head of the pin. His face was so hot he might have been standing before an open fire. He pushed the pin a further half-inch into Eddie's arm, and another small quantity of blood welled up from the base. The pin seemed to be moving in Harry's grasp, pulsing back and forth as if it were breathing.

"Okay," Harry said. "Okay."

He tightened his hold on the pin and pulled. It slipped 43

easily from the wound. Harry held the hat pin before his face just as a doctor holds up a thermometer to read a temperature. He had imagined that the entire bottom section of the shaft would be painted with red, but saw that only a single winding glutinous streak of blood adhered to the pin. For a dizzy second he thought of slipping the end of the pin in his mouth and sucking it clean.

He thought: Maybe in another life I was Lepke Buchalter.

He pulled his handkerchief, a filthy square of red paisley, from his front pocket and wiped the streak of blood from the shaft of the pin. Then he leaned over and gently wiped the red smear from Little Eddie's underarm. Harry refolded the handkerchief so the blood would not show, wiped sweat from his face, and shoved the grubby cloth back into his pocket.

"That was good, Eddie. Now we're going to do something a little bit different."

He knelt down beside his brother and lifted Eddie's nearly weightless, delicately veined arm. "You still can't feel a thing in this arm, Eddie, it's completely numb. It's sound asleep and it won't wake up until I tell it to." Harry repositioned himself in order to hold himself steady while he knelt, and put the point of the hat pin nearly flat against Eddie's arm. He pushed it forward far enough to raise a wrinkle of flesh. The point of the hat pin dug into Eddie's skin but did not break it. Harry pushed harder, and the hat pin raised the little bulge of skin by a small but appreciable amount.

Skin was a lot tougher to break through than anyone imagined.

The pin was beginning to hurt his fingers, so Harry opened his hand and positioned the head against the base of his middle finger, Grimacing, he pushed his hand against the pin. The point of the pin popped through the raised wrinkle.

"Eddie, you're made out of beer cans," Harry said, and tugged the head of the pin backward. The wrinkle flattened out. Now Harry could shove the pin forward again, sliding the shaft deeper and deeper under the surface of Little Eddie's skin. He could see the raised line of the hat pin marching down his brother's arm, looking as prominent as the damage done to a cartoon lawn by a cartoon rabbit. When the mother-of-pearl head was perhaps three inches from the entry hole, Harry pushed it down into Little Eddie's flesh, thus raising the point of the pin. He gave the head a sharp jab, and the point appeared at the end of the ridge in Eddie's skin, poking through a tiny smear of blood. Harry shoved the pin in further. Now it showed about an inch and a half of gray metal at either end.

"Feel anything?"

"Nothing."

Harry juggled the head of the pin, and a bubble of

blood walked out of the entry wound and began to slide down Eddie's arm. Harry sat down on the attic floor beside Eddie and regarded his work. His mind seemed pleasantly empty of thought, filled only with a variety of sensations. He *felt* but could not hear a buzzing in his head, and a blurry film seemed to cover his eyes. He breathed through his mouth. The long pin stuck through Little Eddie's arm looked monstrous seen one way; seen another, it was sheerly beautiful. Skin, blood, and metal. Harry had never seen anything like it before. He reached out and twisted the pin, causing another little blood-snail to crawl from the exit wound. Harry saw all this as if through smudgy glasses, but he did not mind. He knew the blurriness was only mental. He touched the head of the pin again and moved it from side to side. A little more blood leaked from both punctures. Then Harry shoved the pin in, partially withdrew it so that the point nearly disappeared back into Eddie's arm, moved it forward again; and went on like this, back and forth, back and forth as if he was sewing his brother up, for some time.

Finally he withdrew the pin from Eddie's arm. Two long streaks of blood had nearly reached his brother's wrist. Harry ground the heels of his hands into his eyes, blinked, and discovered that his vision had cleared.

He wondered how long he and Eddie had been in the attic. It could have been hours. He could not quite remember what had happened before he had slid the hat pin into Eddie's skin. Now his blurriness really was mental, not visual. A loud uncomfortable pulse beat in his temples. Again he wiped the blood from Eddie's arm. Then he stood on wobbling knees and returned to his chair.

"How's your arm feel, Eddie?"

"Numb," Eddie said in his gravelly sleepy voice.

"The numbness is going away now. Very very slowly. You are beginning to feel your arm again, and it feels very good. There is no pain. It feels like the sun was shining on it all afternoon. It's strong and healthy. Feeling is coming back into your arm, and you can move your fingers and everything."

When he had finished speaking Harry leaned back against the chair and closed his eyes. He rubbed his forehead with his hand and wiped the moisture off on his shirt.

"How does your arm feel?" he said without opening his eyes.

"Good."

"That's great, Little Eddie." Harry flattened his palms against his flushed face, wiped his cheeks and opened his eyes.

I can do this every night, he thought. I can bring Little Eddie up her every single night, at least until school starts.

"Eddie, you're getting stronger and stronger every day. 47

This is really helping you. And the more we do it the stronger you'll get. Do you understand me?"

"I understand you," Eddie said.

"We're almost done for the tonight. There's just one more thing I want to try. But you have to be really deep asleep for this to work. So I want you to go deeper and deeper, as deep as you can go. Relax, and now you are really deep asleep, deep deep, and relaxed and ready and feeling good."

Little Eddie sat sprawled in his chair with his head tilted back and his eyes closed. Two tiny dark spots of blood stood out like mosquito bites on his lower right forearm.

"When I talk to you, Eddie, you're slowly getting younger and younger, you're going backward in time, so now you're not nine years old anymore, you're eight, it's last year and you're in the third grade, and now you're seven, and now you're six years old . . . and now you're five, Eddie, and it's the day of your fifth birthday. You're five years old today, Little Eddie. How old are you?"

"I'm five." To Harry's surprised pleasure, Little Eddie's voice actually seemed younger, as did his hunched posture in the chair.

"How do you feel?"

"Not good. I hate my present. It's terrible. Dad got it, and Mom says it should never be allowed in the house because it's just junk. I wish I wouldn't ever have to have birthdays, they're so terrible. I'm gonna cry."

His face contracted. Harry tried to remember what Eddie had gotten for his fifth birthday, but could not—he caught only a dim memory of shame and disappointment. "What's your present, Eddie?"

In a teary voice, Eddie said, "A radio. But it's busted and Mom says it looks like it came from the junkyard. I don't want it anymore. I don't even wanna *see* it."

Yes, Harry thought, yes, yes, yes. He could remember. On Little Eddie's fifth birthday, Edgar Beevers had produced a yellow plastic radio which even Harry had seen was astoundingly ugly. The dial was cracked, and it was marked here and there with brown circular scablike marks where someone had mashed out cigarettes on it.

The radio had long since been buried in the junk room, where it now lay beneath several geological layers of trash.

"Okay, Eddie, you can forget the radio now, because you're going backward again, you're getting younger, you're going backward through being four years old, and now you're three.

He looked with interest at Little Eddie, whose entire demeanor had changed. From being tearfully unhappy, Eddie now demonstrated a self-sufficient good cheer Harry could not ever remember seeing in him. His arms were folded over his chest. He was smiling, and his eyes were bright and clear and childish.

49

"What do you see?" Harry asked.

"Mommy-ommy-om."

"What's she doing?"

"Mommy's at her desk. She's smoking and looking through her papers." Eddie gibbled. "Mommy looks funny. It looks like smoke is coming out of the top of her head." Eddie ducked his chin and hid his smile behind a hand. "Mommy doesn't see me. I can see her, but she doesn't see me. Oh! Mommy works hard! She works hard at her desk!"

Eddie's smile abruptly left his face. His face froze for a second in a comic rubbery absence of expression; then his eyes widened in terror and his mouth went loose and wobbly.

"What happened?" Harry's mouth had gone dry.

"No, Mommy!" Eddie wailed. "Don't, Mommy! I wasn't spying, I wasn't, I promise—" His words broke off into a screech. "NO, MOMMY! DON'T! DON'T!, MOMMY!" Eddie jumped upward, sending his chair flying back, and ran blindly toward the rear of the attic. Harry's head rang with Eddie's screeches. He heard a sharp *crack!* of wood breaking, but only as a small part of all the noise Eddie was making as he charged around the attic. Eddie had run into a tangle of hanging dresses, spun around, enmeshing himself deeper in the dresses, and was now tearing himself away from the web of dresses, pulling some of them off the rack. A long-sleeved purple dress with an enormous lace collar had draped itself around Eddie like a ghostly dance partner, and another dress, of dull red velvet, snaked around his right leg. Eddie screamed again and yanked himself away from the tangle. The entire rack of clothes wobbled and then went over in a mad jangle of sound.

"NO!" he screeched. "HELP!" Eddie ran straight into a big wooden beam marking off one of the eaves, bounced off, and came windmilling toward Harry. Harry knew his brother could not see him.

"Eddie, stop," he said, but Eddie was past hearing him. Harry tired to make Eddie stop by wrapping his arms around him, but Eddie slammed right into him, hitting Harry's chest with a shoulder and knocking his head painfully against Harry's chin; Harry's arms closed on nothing and his eyes lost focus, and Eddie went crashing into the tilting mirror. The mirror yawned over sideways. Harry saw it tilt with dreamlike slowness toward the floor, then in an eyeblink drop and crash. Broken glass sprayed across the attic floor.

"STOP!" Harry yelled. "STAND STILL, EDDIE!"

Eddie came to rest. A ripped and dirty dress of dull red velvet still clung to his right leg. Blood oozed down his temple from an ugly cut above his eye. He was breathing hard, releasing air in little whimpering exhalations.

"Holy shit," Harry said, looking around at the attic. In only a few seconds Eddie had managed to create what looked at first like absolute devastation. Maryrose's ancient dresses lay tangled in a heap of dusty fabrics from which wire hangers skeletally protruded; gray Eddie-sized footprints lay like a pattern over the muted explosion of colors the dresses now created. When the rack had gone over, it had knocked a section the size of a dinner plate out of a round wooden coffee table Maryrose had particularly prized for its being made from a single section of teak—"a single piece of *teak*, the rarest wood in all the world, all the way from Ceylon!" The much-prized mirror lay in hundreds of glittering pieces across the attic floor. With growing horror, Harry saw that the wooden frame had cracked like a bone, showing a bone-pale, shockingly white fracture in the expanse of dark stain.

Harry's blood tipped within his body, nearly tipping him with it, like the mirror. "Oh God oh God oh God."

He turned slowly around. Eddie stood blinking two feet to his side, wiping ineffectually at the blood running from his forehead and now covering most of his left cheek. He looked like an Indian in war paint—a defeated, lost Indian, for his eyes were dim and his head turned aimlessly from side to side.

A few feet from Eddie lay the chair in which he had been sitting. One of its thin curved wooden arms lay beside it, crudely severed. It looked like an insect's leg, Harry thought, like a toy gun.

52   For a moment Harry thought that his face too was red

with blood. He wiped his hand over his forehead and looked at his glistening palm. It was only sweat. His heart beat like a bell. Beside him Eddie said, "Aaah ... what ... ?" The injury to his head had brought him out of the trance.

The dresses were ruined, stepped-on, tangled, torn. The mirror was broken. The table had been mutilated. Maryrose's chair lay on its side like a murder victim, its severed arm ending in a bristle of snapped ligaments.

"My head *hurts*," Eddie said in a weak, trembling voice. "What happened? Aaah! I'm all blood! I'm all blood, Harry!"

"You're all blood, you're all blood?" Harry shouted at him. "Everything's *all blood*, you dummy! Look around!" He did not recognize his own voice, which sounded high and tinny and seemed to be coming from somewhere else. Little Eddie took an aimless step away from him, and Harry wanted to fly at him, to pound his bloody head into a pancake, to destroy him, smash him. . . .

Eddie held up his bloodstained palm and stared at it. He wiped it vaguely across the front of his T-shirt and took another wandering step. "I'm ascared, Harry," his tiny voice uttered.

"Look what you did!" Harry screamed. "You wrecked everything! Damn it! What do you think is going to happen to us?"

"What's Mom going to do?" Eddie asked in a voice only slightly above a whisper.

"You don't know? Harry yelled. "You're dead!"

Eddie started to weep.

Harry bunched his hands into fists and clamped his eyes shut. They were both dead, that was the real truth. Harry opened his eyes, which felt hot and oddly heavy, and stared at his sobbing, red-smeared, useless little brother. "Blue rose," he said.

10

Little Eddie's hands fell to his sides. His chin dropped, and his mouth fell open. Blood ran in a smooth wide band down the left side of his face, dipped under the line of his jaw, and continued on down his neck and into his T-shirt. Pooled blood in his left eyebrow dripped steadily onto the floor, as if from a faucet.

"You are going deep *asleep*," Harry said. Where was the hat pin? He looked back to the single standing chair and saw the mother-of-pearl head glistening on the floor near it. "Your whole body is *numb*." He moved over to the pin, bent down, and picked it up. The metal shaft felt warm in his fingers. "You can feel no *pain*." He went back to

Little Eddie. "Nothing can *hurt* you." Harry's breath seemed to be breathing itself, forcing itself into his throat in hot harsh shallow pants, then expelling itself out.

"Did you *hear* me, Little Eddie?"

In his gravelly, slow-moving hypnotized voice, Little Eddie said, "I heard you."

"And you can feel no *pain?*"

"I can feel no pain."

Harry drew his arm back, the point of the hat pin extending forward from his fist, and then jerked his hand forward as hard as he could and stuck the pin into Eddie's abdomen right through the blood-soaked T-shirt. He exhaled sharply, and tasted a sour misery on his breath.

"You don't feel a thing."

"I don't feel a thing."

Harry opened his right hand and drove his palm against the head of the pin, hammering it in another few inches. Little Eddie looked like a voodoo doll. A kind of sparkling light surrounded him, Harry gripped the head of the pin with his thumb and forefinger and yanked it out. He held it up and inspected it. Glittering light surrounded the pin too. The long shaft was painted with blood. Harry slipped the point into his mouth and closed his lips around the warm metal.

He saw himself, a man in another life, standing in a row with men like himself in a bleak gray landscape defined by barbed wire. Emaciated people in rags shuffled 55 up toward them and spat on their clothes. The smells of dead flesh and of burning flesh hung in the air. Then the vision was gone, and Little Eddie stood before him again, surrounded by layers of glittering light.

Harry grimaced or grinned, he could not have told the difference, and drove his long spike deep into Eddie's stomach.

Eddie uttered a small *Oof.*

"You don't feel anything, Eddie," Harry whispered. "You feel good all over. You never felt better in your life."

"Never felt better in my life."

Harry slowly pulled out the pin and cleaned it with his fingers.

He was able to remember every single thing anyone had ever told him about Tommy Golz.

"Now you're going to play a funny, funny game," he said. "This is called the Tommy Golz game because it's going to keep you safe from Mrs. Franken. Are you ready?" Harry carefully slid the pin into the fabric of his shirt collar, all the while watching Eddie's slack blood-streaked person. Vibrating bands of light beat rhythmically and steadily about Eddie's face.

"Ready," Eddie said.

"I'm going to give you your instructions now, Little Eddie. Pay attention to everything I say and it's all going to be okay. Everything's going to be okay—as long as you play the game exactly the way I tell you. You understand, don't you?"

"I understand."

"Tell me what I just said."

"Everything's gonna be okay as long as I play the game exactly the way you tell me." A dollop of blood slid off Eddie's eyebrow and splashed onto his already soaked T-shirt.

"Good, Eddie. Now the first thing you do is fall down—not now, when I tell you. I'm going to give you all the instructions, and then I'm going to count backwards from ten, and when I get to *one*, you'll start playing the game. Okay?"

"Okay.

"So first you fall down, Little Eddie. You fall down real hard. Then comes the fun part of the game. You bang your head on the floor. You start to go crazy. You twitch, and you bang your hands and feet on the floor. You do that for a long time. I guess you do that until you count to about a hundred. You foam at the mouth, you twist all over the place. You get real stiff, and then you get real loose, and then you get real stiff, and then real loose again, and all this time you're banging your head and your hands and feet on the floor, and you're twisting all over the place. Then when you finish counting to a hundred in your head, you do the last thing. You swallow your tongue. And that's the game. When you swallow 57 your tongue you're the winner. And then nothing bad can happen to you, and Mrs. Franken won't be able to hurt you ever ever ever."

Harry stopped talking. His hands were shaking. After a second he realized that his insides were shaking too. He raised his trembling fingers to his shirt collar and felt the hat pin.

"Tell me how you win the game, Little Eddie. What's the last thing you do?"

"I swallow my tongue."

"Right. And then Mrs. Franken and Mom will never be able to hurt you, because you won the game."

"Good," said Little Eddie. The glittering light shimmered about him.

"Okay, we'll start playing right now," Harry said. "Ten." He went toward the attic steps. "Nine." He reached the steps. "Eight."

He went down one step. "Seven." Harry descended another two steps. "Six." When he went down another two steps, he called up in a slightly louder voice, "Five."

Now his head was beneath the level of the attic floor, and he could not see Little Eddie anymore. All he could hear was the soft, occasional plop of liquid hitting the floor.

"Four."

"Three."

"Two." He was now at the door to the attic steps.

Harry opened the door, stepped through it, breathed hard, and shouted "One!" up the stairs.

He heard a thud, and then quickly closed the door behind him.

Harry went across the hall and into the "dormitory" bedroom. There seemed to be a strange absence of light in the hallway. For a second he saw—was sure he saw—a line of dark trees across a wall of barbed wire. Harry closed this door behind him too, and went to his narrow bed and sat down. He could feel blood beating in his face; his eyes seemed oddly warm, as if they were heated by filaments. Harry slowly, almost reverently, extracted the hat pin from his collar and set it on his pillow. "A hundred," he said. "Ninety-nine, ninety-eight, ninety-seven, ninety-six, ninety-five, ninety-four . . ."

When he had counted down to *"one,"* he stood up and left the bedroom. He went quickly downstairs without looking at the door behind which lay the attic steps. One the ground floor he slipped into Maryrose's bedroom, crossed over to her desk, and slip open the bottom right-hand drawer. From the drawer he took a velvet-covered box. This he opened, and jabbed the hat pin in the ball of material, studded with pins of all sized and descriptions, from which he had taken it. He replaced the box in the drawer, pushed the drawer into the desk, and quickly left the room and went upstairs.

Back in his own bedroom, Harry took off his clothes and climbed into his bed. His face still burned.

He must have fallen asleep very quickly, because the next thing he knew Albert was slamming his way into the bedroom and tossing his clothes and boots all over the place. "You asleep?" Albert asked. "You left the attic light on, you fuckin' dummies, but if you think I'm gonna save your fuckin' asses and go up and turn it off, you're even stupider than you look."

Harry was careful not to move a finger, not to move even a hair.

He held his breath while Albert threw himself onto his bed, and when Albert's breathing relaxed and slowed, Harry followed his big brother into sleep. He did not awaken again until he heard his father half-screeching, half-sobbing up in the attic, and that was very late at night.

II

Sonny came from Fort Sill, George all the way from Germany. Between them, they held up a sodden Edgar Beevers at the grave site while a minister Harry had never seen before read from a Bible as cracked and rubbed as an old brown shoe. Between his two older sons, Harry's father looked bent and ancient, a skinny old man only steps from the grave himself. Sonny and George despised their father, Harry saw—they held him up on sufferance, in part because they had chipped in thirty dollars apiece to buy him a suit and did not want to see it collapse with its owner inside onto the lumpy clay of the graveyard. His whiskers glistened in the sun, and moisture shone beneath his eyes and at the corners of his mouth. He had been shaking too severely for either Sonny or George to shave him, and had been capable of moving in a straight line only after George let him take a couple of long swallows from a leather-covered flask he took out of his duffel bag.

The minister uttered a few sage words on the subject of epilepsy.

Sonny and George looked as solid as brick walls in their uniforms, like prison guards or actual prisons themselves. Next to them, Albert looked shrunken and unfinished. Albert wore the green plaid sport jacket in which he had graduated from the eighth grade, and his wrists hung prominent and red four inches below the bottoms of the sleeves. His motorcycle boots were visible beneath his light gray trousers, but they, like the green jacket, had lost their flash. Like Albert, too: ever since the discovery of Eddie's body, Albert had gone around the house looking as if he'd just bitten off the end of his tongue and was 61 trying to decide whether or not to spit it out. He never looked anybody in the eye, and he rarely spoke. Albert acted as though a gigantic padlock had been fixed to the middle of his chest and *he* was damned if he'd ever take it off. He had not asked Sonny or George a single question about the Army. Every now and then he would utter a remark about the gas station so toneless that it suffocated any reply.

Harry looked at Albert standing beside their mother, kneading his hands together and keeping his eyes fixed as if by decree on the square foot of ground before him. Albert glanced over at Harry, knew he was being looked at, and did what to Harry was an extraordinary thing. Albert *froze.* All expression drained out of his face, and his hands locked immovably together. He looked as little able to see or hear as a statue. *He's that way because he told Little Eddie that he wished he would die,* Harry thought for the tenth or eleventh time since he had realized this, and with undiminished awe. Then was he lying? Harry wondered. And if he really did wish that Little Eddie would drop dead, why isn't he happy now? Didn't he get what he wanted? Albert would never spit out that piece of his tongue, Harry thought, watching his brother blink slowly and sightlessly toward the ground.

Harry shifted his gaze uneasily to his father, still propped up between George and Sonny, heard that the 62 minister was finally reaching the end of his speech, and took a fast look at his mother. Maryrose was standing very straight in a black dress and black sunglasses, holding the straps of her bag in front of her with both hands. Except for the color of her clothes, she could have been a spectator at a tennis match. Harry knew by the way she was holding her face that she was wishing she could smoke. Dying for a cigarette, he thought, ha ha, the Monster Mash, it's a graveyard smash.

The minister finished speaking, and made a rhetorical gesture with his hands. The coffin sank on ropes into the rough earth. Harry's father began to weep loudly. First George, then Sonny, picked up large damp shovel-marked pieces of the clay and dropped them on the coffin. Edgar Beevers nearly fell in after his own tiny clod, but George contemptuously swung him back. Maryrose marched forward, bent and picked up a random piece of clay with thumb and forefinger as if using tweezers, dropped it, and turned away before it stuck. Albert fixed his eyes on Harry—his own clod had split apart in his hand and crumbled away between his fingers. Harry shook his head *no*. He did not want to drop dirt on Eddie's coffin and make that noise. He did not want to look at Eddie's coffin again. There was enough dirt around to do the job without him hitting that metal box like he was trying to ring Eddie's doorbell. He stepped back.

"Mom says we have to get back to the house," Albert said.

Maryrose lit up as soon as they got into the single black car they had rented through the funeral parlor, and breathed out acrid smoke over everybody crowded into the backseat. The car backed into a narrow graveyard lane, and turned down the main road toward the front gates.

In the front seat, next to the driver, Edgar Beevers drooped sideways and leaned his head against the window, leaving a blurred streak on the glass.

"How in the name of hell could Little Eddie have epilepsy without anybody knowing about it?" George asked.

Albert stiffened and stared out the window.

"Well, that's epilepsy," Maryrose said. "Eddie could have gone on for years without having an attack." That she worked in a hospital always gave her remarks of this sort a unique gravity, almost as if she were a doctor.

"Must have been some fit," Sonny said, squeezed into place between Harry and Albert.

"*Grand mal,*" Maryrose said, and took another hungry drag on her cigarette.

"Poor little bastard," George said. "Sorry, Mom."

"I know you're in the Armed Forces, and Armed Forces people speak very freely, but I wish you would not use that kind of language."

Harry, jammed into Sonny's rock-hard side, felt his brother's body twitch with a hidden laugh, though Sonny's face did not alter.

"I said I was sorry, Mom," George said.

"Yes. Driver! Driver!" Maryrose was leaning forward, reaching out one claw to tap the chauffeur's shoulder. "Livermore is the next right. Do you know South Sixth Street?"

"I'll get you there," the driver said.

This is not my family, Harry thought. I came from somewhere else and my rules are different from theirs.

His father mumbled something inaudible as soon as they got in the door and disappeared into his curtained-off cubicle. Maryrose put her sunglasses in her purse and marched into the kitchen to warm the coffeecake and the macaroni casserole, both made that morning, in the oven. Sonny and George wandered into the living room and sat down on opposite ends of the couch. They did not look at each other—George picked up a *Reader's Digest* from the table and began leafing through it backward, and sonny folded his hands in his lap and stared at his thumbs. Albert's footsteps plodded up the stairs, crossed the landing, and went into the dormitory bedroom.

"What's she in the kitchen for?" Sonny asked, speaking to his hands. "Nobody's going to come. Nobody ever comes here, because she never wanted them to."

"Albert's taking this kind of hard, Harry," George said He propped the magazine against the stiff folds of his uniform and looked across the room at his little brother. 65

Harry had seated himself beside the door, as out of the way as possible. George's attentions rather frightened him, though George had behaved with consistent kindness ever since his arrival two days after Eddie's death. His crew cut still bristled and he could still break rocks with his chin, but some violent demon seemed to have left him. "You think he'll be okay?"

"Him? Sure." Harry tilted his head, grimaced.

"He didn't see Little Eddie first, did he?"

"No, Dad did," Harry said. "He saw the light on in the attic when he came home, I guess. Albert went up there, though. I guess there was so much blood Dad thought somebody broke in and killed Eddie. But he just bumped his head, and that's where the blood came from."

"Head wounds bleed like bastards," Sonny said. "A guy hit me with a bottle once in Tokyo, I thought I was gonna bleed to death right there."

"And Mom's stuff got all messed up?" George asked quietly.

This time Sonny looked up.

"Pretty much, I guess. The dress rack got knocked down. Dad cleaned up what he could, the next day. One of the cane-back chairs got broke, and a hunk got knocked out of the teak table. And the mirror got broken into a million pieces."

Sonny shook his head, and made a soft whistling sound 66 through his pursed lips.

"She's a tough old gal," George said. "I hear her coming though, so we have to stop, Harry. But we can talk tonight."

Harry nodded.

12

After dinner that night, when Maryrose had gone to bed—the hospital had given her two nights off—Harry sat across the kitchen table from a George who clearly had something to say. Sonny had polished off a six-pack by himself in front of the television and gone up to the dormitory bedroom by himself. Albert had disappeared shortly after dinner, and their father had never emerged from his cubicle beside the junk room.

"I'm glad Pete Petrosian came over," George said. "He's a good old boy. Ate two helpings, too."

Harry was startled by George's use of their neighbor's first name—he was not even sure that he had ever heard it before.

Mr. Petrosian had been their only caller that afternoon. Harry had seen that his mother was grateful that someone had come, and despite her preparations wanted no more company after Mr. Petrosian had left.

"Think I'll get a beer, that is if Sonny didn't drink it all," George said, and stood up and opened the fridge. His uniform looked as if it had been painted on his body, and his muscles bulged and moved like a horse's. "Two left," he said. "Good thing you're underage." George popped the caps off both bottles and came back to the table. He winked at Harry, then tilted the first bottle to his lips and took a good swallow. "So what the devil was Little Eddie doing up there, anyhow? Trying on dresses?"

"I don't know," Harry said. "I was asleep."

"Hell, I know I kind of lost touch with Little Eddie, but I got the impression he was scared of his own shadow. I'm surprised he had the nerve to go up there and mess around with Mom's precious stuff."

"Yeah," Harry said. "Me too."

"You didn't happen to go with him, did you?" George tilted the bottle to his mouth and winked at Harry again.

Harry just looked back. He could feel his face getting hot.

"I just was thinking maybe you saw it happen to Little Eddie, and got too scared to tell anybody. Nobody would be mad at you, Harry. Nobody would blame your for anything. You couldn't know how to help someone who's having an epileptic fit. Little Eddie swallowed his tongue. Even if you'd been standing next to him when he did it and had the presence of mind to call an ambulance, he would have died before it got there. Unless you knew what was wrong and how to correct it. Which nobody would expect you to know, not in a million years. Nobody'd blame you for anything, Harry, not even Mom."

"I was asleep," Harry said.

"Okay, okay. I just wanted you to know."

They sat in silence for a time, then both spoke at once.

"Did you know—"

"We had this—"

"Sorry," George said, "Go on."

"Did you know that Dad used to be in the Army? In World War II?"

"Yeah, I knew that. Of course I knew that."

"Did you know that he committed the perfect murder once?"

"*What?*"

"Dad committed the perfect murder. When he was at Dachau, that death camp."

"Oh, Christ, is that what you're talking about? You got a funny way of seeing things, Harry. He shot an enemy who was trying to escape. That's not murder, it's war. There's one hell of a big difference."

"I'd like to see war someday," Harry said. "I'd like to be in the Army, like you and Dad."

"Hold your horses, hold your horses," George said, smiling now. "That's sort of one of the things I wanted to talk to you about." He set down his beer bottle, cradled his hands around it, and tilted his head to look at Harry.

This was obviously going to be serious. "You know, I used to be crazy and stupid, that's the only way to put it. I used to look for fights. I had a chip on my shoulder the size of a house, and pounding some dipshit into a coma was my idea of a great time. The Army did me a lot of good. It made me grow up. But I don't think you need that, Harry. You're too smart for that—if you have to go, you go, but out of all of us, you're the one who could really amount to something in this world. You could be a doctor. Or a lawyer. You ought to get the best education you can, Harry. What you have to do is stay out of trouble and get to college."

"Oh, college," Harry said.

"Listen to me, Harry. I make pretty good money, and I got nothing to spend it on. I'm not going to get married and have kids, that's for sure. So I want to make you a proposition. If you keep your nose clean and make it through high school, I'll help you out with college. Maybe you can get a scholarship—I think you're smart enough, Harry, and a scholarship would be great. But either way, I'll see you make it through." George emptied the first bottle, set it down, and gave Harry a quizzical look. "Let's get one person in this family off on the right track. What do you say?"

"I guess I better keep reading," Harry said.

"I hope you'll read your ass off, little buddy," George said, and picked up the second bottle of beer.

13

The day after Sonny left, George put all of Eddie's toys and clothes into a box and squeezed the box into the junk room; two days later, George took a bus to New York so he could get his flight to Munich from Idlewild. An hour before he caught his bus, George walked Harry up to Big John's and stuffed him full of hamburgers and french fries and said, "You'll probably miss Eddie a lot, won't you?" "I guess," Harry said, but the truth was that Eddie was now only a vacancy, a blank space. Sometimes a door would close and Harry would know that Little Eddie had just come in; but when he turned to look, he saw only emptiness. George's question, asked a week ago, was the last time Harry had heard anyone pronounce his brother's name.

In the seven days since the charmed afternoon at Big John's and the departure on a southbound bus of George Beevers, everything seemed to have gone back to the way it was before, but Harry knew that really everything had changed. They had been a loose, divided family of five, two parents and three sons. Now they seemed to be a family of three, and Harry thought that the actual truth was that the family had shrunk down to two, himself and his mother.

Edgar Beevers had left home—he too was an absence. After two visits from policemen who parked their cars right outside the house, after listening to his mother's muttered expressions of disgust, after the spectacle of his pale, bleary, but sober and clean-shaven father trying over and over to knot a necktie in front of the bathroom mirror, Harry finally accepted that his father had been caught shoplifting. His father had to go to court, and he was scared. His hands shook so uncontrollably that he could not shave himself, and in the end Maryrose had to knot his tie—doing it in one, two, three quick movements as brutal as the descent of a knife, never removing the cigarette from her mouth.

GRIEF-STRICKEN AREA MAN FORGIVEN OF SHOPLIFTING CHARGE, read the headline over the little story in the evening newspaper which at last explained his father's crime. Edgar Beevers had been stopped on the sidewalk outside the Livermore Avenue National Tea, T-bone steaks hidden inside his shirt and a bottle of Rhinegold beer in each of his front pockets. He had stolen two steaks! He had put beer bottles in his pockets! This made Harry feel like he was sweating inside. The judge had sent him home, but home was not where he went. For a short time, Harry thought, his father had hung out on Oldtown Road, Palmyra's skid row, and slept in vacant lots with winos and bums. (Then a woman was supposed to have taken him in.)

Albert was another mystery. It was as though a creature from outer space had taken him over and was using his body, like *Invasion of the Body Snatchers*. Albert looked like he thought somebody was always standing behind him, watching every move he made. He was still carrying around that piece of his tongue, and pretty soon, Harry thought, he'd get so used to it that he would forget he had it.

Three days after George left Palmyra, Albert actually tagged along after Harry on the way to Big John's. Harry turned around on the sidewalk and saw Albert in his black jeans and grease-blackened T-shirt halfway down the block, shoving his hands in his pockets and looking hard at the ground. That was Albert's way of pretending to be invisible. The next time he turned around, Albert growled, "Keep walking."

Harry went to work on the pinball machine as soon as he got inside Big John's. Albert slunk in a few minutes later and went straight to the counter. He took one of the stained paper menus from a stack squeezed in beside a napkin dispenser and inspected it as if he had never seen it before.

"Hey, let me introduce you guys," said Big John, leaning against the far side of the counter. Like Albert, he wore black jeans and motorcycle boots but his dark hair, 73 daringly for the nineteen fifties, fell over his ears. Beneath his stained white apron he wore a long-sleeved black shirt with a pattern of tiny azure palm trees. "You two are the Beevers boys, Harry and Bucky. Say hello to each other, fellows."

Bucky Beaver was a toothy rodent in an Ipana television commercial. Albert blushed, still grimly staring at his menu sheet.

"Call me 'Beans,'" Harry said, and felt Albert's gaze shift wonderingly to him.

"Beans and Bucky, the Beevers boys," Big John said. "Well, Buck, what'll you have?"

"Hamburger, fries, shake," Albert said.

Big John half-turned and yelled the order through the hatch to Mama Mary's kitchen. For a time the three of them stood in uneasy silence. Then Big John said, "Heard your old man found a new place to hang his hat. His new girlfriend is a real pistol, I heard. Spent some time in County Hospital. On account of she picked up little messages from outer space on the good old Philco. You hear that?"

"He's gonna come home real soon," Harry said. "He doesn't have any new girlfriend. He's staying with an old friend. She's a rich lady and she wants to help him out because she knows he had a lot of trouble and she's going to get him a real good job, and then he'll come home, and we'll be able to move to a better house and everything."

He never even saw Albert move, but Albert had materialized beside him. Fury, rage, and misery distorted his face. Harry had time to cry out only once, and then Albert slammed a fist into his chest and knocked him backward into the pinball machine.

"I bet that felt real good," Harry said, unable to keep down his own rage. "I bet you'd like to kill me, Huh? Huh, Albert? How about that?"

Albert moved backward two paces and lowered his hands, already looking impassive, locked into himself.

For a second in which his breath failed and dazzling light filled his eyes, Harry saw Little Eddie's slack, trusting face before him. Then Big John came up from nowhere with a big hamburger and a mound of french fries on a plate and said, "Down, boys. Time for Rocky here to tackle his dinner."

That night Albert said nothing at all to Harry as they lay in their beds. Neither did he fall asleep. Harry knew that for most of the night Albert just closed his eyes and faked it, like a possum in trouble. Harry tired to stay awake long enough to see when Albert's fake sleep melted into the real thing, but he sank into dreams long before that.

He was rushing down the stony corridor of a castle past suits of armor and torches guttering in sconces. His bladder was bursting, he had to let go, he could not hold it more than another few seconds. . . . At last he came to the open bathroom door and ran into that splendid gleaming place. He began to tug at his zipper, and looked around for the butler and the row of marble urinals. Then he froze. Little Eddie was standing before him, not the uniformed butler. Blood ran in a gaudy streak from a gash high on his forehead over his cheek and right down his neck, neat as paint. Little Eddie was waving frantically at Harry, his eyes bright and hysterical, his mouth working soundlessly because he had swallowed his tongue.

Harry sat up straight in bed, about to scream, then realized that the bedroom was all around him and Little Eddie was gone. He hurried downstairs to the bathroom.

14

At two o'clock the next afternoon Harry Beevers had to pee again, and just as badly, but this time he was a long way from the bathroom across from the junk room and his father's old cubicle. Harry was standing in the humid sunlight across the street from 45 Oldtown Way. This short street connected the bums, transient hotels, bars, and seedy movie theaters of Oldtown Road with the more 76 respectable hotels, department stores, and restaurants of

Palmyra Avenue—the real downtown. Forty-five Oldtown Way was a four-story brick tenement with an exoskeleton of fire escapes. Black iron bars covered the ground-floor windows. On one side of 45 Oldtown Way were the large soap-smeared windows of a bankrupted shoe store, on the other a vacant lot where loose bricks and broken bottles nestled amongst dandelions and tall Queen Anne's lace. Harry's father lived in that building now. Everybody else knew it, and since Big John had told him, now Harry knew it too.

He jigged from leg to leg, waiting for a woman to come out through the front door. It was as chipped and peeling as his own, and a broken fanlight sat drunkenly atop it. Harry checked the row of dented mailboxes on the brick wall just outside the door for his father's name, but none bore any names at all. Big John hadn't known the name of the woman who had taken Harry's father in, but he said that she was large, black-haired, and crazy, and that she had two children in foster care. About half an hour ago a dark-haired woman had come through the door, but Harry had not followed her because she had not looked especially large to him. Now he was beginning to have doubts. What did Big John mean by "large," anyhow? As big as he was? And how could you tell if someone was crazy? Did it show? Maybe he should have followed that woman. This thought made him even more anxious, and he squeezed his legs together.

His father was in that building now, he thought. Harry thought of his father lying on an unmade bed, his brown winter coat around him, his hat pulled how on his forehead like Lepke Buchalter's, drawing on a cigarette, looking moodily out the window.

Then he had to pee so urgently that he could not have held it in for more than a few seconds, and trotted across the street and into the vacant lot. Near the back fence the tall weeds gave him some shelter from the street. He frantically unzipped and let the braided yellow stream splash into a nest of broken bricks. Harry looked up at the side of the building beside him. It looked very tall, and seemed to be tilting slightly toward him. The four blank windows on each floor looked back down at him. Just as he was tugging at his zipper, he heard the front door of the building slam shut.

His heart slammed too. Harry hunkered down behind the tall white weeds. Anxiety that she might walk the other way, toward downtown, made him twine his fingers together and bend his fingers back. If he waited about five seconds, he figured, he'd know she was going toward Palmyra Avenue and would be able to get across the lot in time to see which way she turned. His knuckles cracked. He felt like a soldier hiding in a forest, like a murder weapon.

He raised up on his toes and got ready to dash back
across the street, because an empty grocery cart closely

followed by a moving belly with a tiny head and basketball shoes, a cigar tilted in its mouth like a flag, appeared past the front of the building. He could go back and wait across the street. Harry settled down and watched the stomach go down the sidewalk past him. Then a shadow separated itself from the street side of the fat man, and the shadow became a black-haired woman in a long loose dress now striding past the grocery cart. She shook back her head, and Harry saw that she was tall as a queen and that her skin was darker than olive. Deep lines cut through her cheeks. It had to be the woman who had taken his father in. Her long rapid strides had taken her well past the fat man's grocery cart. Harry ran across the rubble of the lot and began to follow her up the sidewalk.

His father's woman walked in a hard, determined way. She stepped down into the street to get around groups too slow for her. At the Oldtown Road corner she wove her way through a group of saggy-bottomed men passing around a bottle in a paper bag and cut in front of two black children dribbling a basketball up the street. She was on the move, and Harry had to hurry along to keep her in sight.

"I bet you don't believe me," he said to himself, practicing, and skirted the group of winos on the corner. He picked up his speed until he was nearly trotting. The two black kids with the basketball ignored him as he kept pace with them, then went on ahead. Far up the block, the tall 79 woman with bouncing black hair marched right past a flashing neon sign in a bar window. Her bottom moved back and forth in the loose dress, surprisingly big whenever it bulged out the fabric of the dress; her back seemed as long as a lion's. "What would you say if I told you," Harry said to himself.

A block and a half ahead, the woman turned on her heel and went through the door of the A & P store. Harry sprinted the rest of the way, pushed the yellow wooden door marked ENTER, and walked into the dense, humid air of the grocery store. Other A & P stores may have been air-conditioned, but not the little shop on Oldtown Road.

What was foster care, anyway? Did you get money if you gave away your children?

A good person's children would never be in foster care, Harry thought. He saw the woman turning into the third aisle past the cash register. He took in with a small shock that she was taller than his father. If I told you, you might not believe me. He went slowly around the corner of the aisle. She was standing on the pale wooden floor about fifteen feet in front of him, carrying a wire basket in one hand. He stepped forward. What I have to say might seem. For good luck, he touched the hat pin inserted into the bottom of his collar. She was staring at a row of brightly colored bags of potato chips. Harry cleared his throat. The woman reached down and picked up a big bag and put it in the basket.

"Excuse me," Harry said.

She turned her head to look at him. Her face was as wide as it was long, and in the mellow light from the store's low-wattage bulbs her skin seemed a very light shade of brown. Harry knew he was meeting an equal. She looked like she could do magic, as if she could shoot fire and sparks out of her fierce black eyes.

"I bet you don't believe me," he said, "but a kid can hypnotize people just as good as an adult."

"What's that?"

His rehearsed words now sounded crazy to him, but he stuck to his script.

"A kid can hypnotize people. I can hypnotize people. Do you believe that?"

"I don't think I even care," she said, and wheeled away toward the rear of the aisle.

"I bet you don't think I could hypnotize you," Harry said.

"Kid, get lost."

Harry suddenly knew that if he kept talking about hypnotism the woman would turn down the next aisle and ignore him no matter what he said, or else begin to speak in a very loud voice about seeing the manager. "My name is Harry Beevers," he said to her back. "Edgar Beevers is my dad."

She stopped and turned around and looked expressionlessly into his face.

"I wonder if you maybe you call him Beans," Harry said.

"Oh, great," she said. "That's just great. So you're one of his boys. Terrific. *Beans* wants potato chips, what do you want?"

"I want you to fall down and bang your head and swallow your tongue and *die* and get buried and have people drop dirt on you," Harry said. The woman's mouth fell open. "Then I want you to puff up with *gas*. I want you *to rot*. I want you to turn green and *black*. I want your *skin* to slide off your bones."

"You're crazy!" the woman shouted at him. "Your whole family's crazy! Do you think your mother wants him anymore?"

"My father shot us in the back," Harry said, and turned and bolted down the aisle for the door.

Outside, he began to trot down seedy Oldtown Road. At Oldtown Way he turned left. When he ran past number 45, he looked at every blank window. His face, his hands, his whole body felt hot and wet. Soon he had a stitch in his side. Harry blinked, and saw a dark line of trees, a wall of barbed wire before him. At the top of Oldtown Way he turned into Palmyra Avenue. From there he could continue running past Allouette's boarded-up windows, past all the stores old and new, to the corner of Livermore, and from there, he only now realized, to the

little house that belonged to Mr. Petrosian.

15

On a sweltering mid-afternoon eleven years later at a
camp in the central highlands of Vietnam, Lieutenant
Harry Beevers closed the flap of his tent against the mos-
quitos and sat on the edge of his temporary bunk to write
a long-delayed letter back to Pat Caldwell, the young
woman he wanted to marry—and to whom he would be
married for a time, after his return from the war to New
York State.

This is what he wrote, after frequent crossings-out and
hesitations. Harry later destroyed this letter.

Dear Pat:

*First of all I want you to know how much I miss you, my
darling, and that if I ever get out of this beautiful and terrible country, which I am going to do, that I am going to chase
you mercilessly and unrelentingly until you say that you'll
marry me. Maybe in the euphoria of relief (YES!!!), I have
the future all worked out, Pat, and you're a big part of it. I
have eighty-six days until DEROS, when they pat me on the
head and put me on that big bird out of here. Now that my
record is clear again, I have no doubts that Columbia Law*

School will take me in. As you know, my law board scores were pretty respectable (modest me!) when I took them at Adelphi. I'm pretty sure I could even get into Harvard Law, but I settled on Columbia because then we could both be in New York.

My brother George has already told me that he will help out with whatever money I—you and I—will need. George put me through Adelphi. I don't think you knew this. In fact, nobody knew this. When I look back, in college I was such a jerk. I wanted everybody to think my family was well-to-do, or at least middle-class. The truth is, we were damn poor, which I think makes my accomplishments all the more note-worthy, all the more loveworthy!

You see, this experience, even with all the ugly and self-doubting and humiliating moments, has done me a lot of good. I was right to come here, even though I had no idea what it was really like. I think I needed the experience of war to complete me, and I tell you this even though I know that you will detest any such idea. In fact, I have to tell you that a big part of me loves being here, and that in some way, even with all this trouble, this year will always be one of the high points of my life. Pat, as you see I'm determined to be honest—to be an honest man. If I'm going to be a lawyer, I ought to be honest, don't you think? (Or maybe the reverse is the reality!) One thing that has meant a lot to me here has been what I can only call the close comrade-ship of my friends and my men—I actually like the grunts more than the usual officer types, which of course means that I get more loyalty and better performance from my men than the usual lieutenant. Someday I'd like you to meet Mike Poole and Tim Underhill and Pumo the Puma and the most amazing of all, M.O. Dengler, who of course was involved with me in the Ia Thuc cave incident. These guys stuck by me. I even have a nickname, "Beans." They call me "Beans" Beevers, and I like it.

There was no way my court-martial could have really put me in any trouble, because all the facts, and my own men, were on my side. Besides, could you see me actually killing children? This is Vietnam and you kill people, that's what we're doing here—we kill Charlies. But we don't kill babies and children. Not even in the heat of wartime—and Ia Thuc was pretty hot!

Well, this is my way of letting you know that at the court-martial of course I received a complete and utter vindication. Dengler did too. There were even unofficial mutterings about giving us medals for all the BS we put up with for the past six weeks—including that amazing story in Time magazine. Before people start yelling about atrocities, they ought to have all the facts straight. Fortunately, last week's magazines go out with the rest of the trash.

Besides, I already knew too much about what death does to people.

I never told you that I once had a little brother named Edward. When I was ten, my little brother wandered up into the top floor of our house one night and suffered a fatal epileptic fit. This event virtually destroyed my family. It led directly to my father's leaving home. (He had been a hero in WWII, something else I never told you.) It deeply

85

changed, I would say even damaged, my older brother Albert. Albert tried to enlist in 1964, but they wouldn't take him because they said he was psychologically unfit. My mom too almost came apart for a while. She used to go up in the attic and cry and wouldn't come down. So you could say that my family was pretty well destroyed, or ruined, or whatever you want to call it, by a sudden death. I took it, and my dad's desertion, pretty hard myself. You don't get over these things easily.

The court-martial lasted exactly four hours. Big deal, hey?, as we used to say back in Palmyra. We used to have a neighbor named Pete Petrosian who said things like that, and against what must have been million-to-one odds, died exactly the same way my brother did, about two weeks after—lightning really did strike twice. I guess it's dumb to think about him now, but maybe one thing war does is to make you conversant with death. How it happens, what it does to people, what it means, how all the dead in your life are somehow united, joined, part of your eternal family. This is a profound feeling, Pat, and no damn whipped-up failed court-martial can touch it. If there were any innocent children in that cave, then they are in my family forever, like little Edward and Pete Petrosian, and the rest of my life is a poem to them. But the Army says there weren't, and so do I.

I love you and love you and love you. You can stop worrying now and start thinking about being married to a Columbia Law student with one hell of a good future. I won't tell you any more war stories than you want to hear. And

*that's a promise, whether the stories are about Nam or Pal-
myra.*

> *Always yours,*
> *Harry*
> *(aka "Beans!")*

PENGUIN 60s

are published on the occasion of Penguin's 60th anniversary

FOR THE BEST IN PAPERBACKS, LOOK FOR THE 🐧